THIS WALKER BOOK BELONGS TO:

laughing

aching

pushing

pouring

chatting

hopping

sulking

kissing

sneezing

hammering

pretending

dribbling

swinging

chatting

blowing

building

resting

catching

For Brenda

First published 1994 by Walker Books Ltd
87 Vauxhall Walk, London SE11 5HJ

This edition published 1995

6 8 10 9 7

© 1994 Shirley Hughes

This book has been typeset in Plantin.

Printed in Hong Kong

British Library Cataloguing in Publication Data
A catalogue record for this book is
available from the British Library.

ISBN 0-7445-3654-5

Chatting

Shirley Hughes

WALKER BOOKS
AND SUBSIDIARIES
LONDON • BOSTON • SYDNEY

I like chatting.

I chat to the cat,

and I chat in the car.

I chat with friends in the park,

and to the lady at the supermarket.

Grown-ups like chatting too.

Sometimes these chats go on
for rather a long time.

The lady next door is
an especially good chatterer.

When Mum is busy she says that there are just too many chatterboxes around.

So I go off and chat to Bemily –
but she never says a word.

The baby likes

a chat on his

toy telephone.

He makes

a lot of calls.

But I can chat
to Grandma
and Grandpa
on the real
telephone.

Some of the best chats
of all are with Dad,

when he comes to
say good night.

laughing

aching

pushing

pouring

chatting

hopping

sulking

kissing

sneezing

hammering

pretending

dribbling

swinging

chatting

blowing

building

resting

catching

MORE WALKER PAPERBACKS
For You to Enjoy

Also by Shirley Hughes

BOUNCING / CHATTING / GIVING / HIDING

Each of the books in this series for pre-school children takes a single everyday verb and entertainingly shows some of its many meanings and applications.

"There's so much to look at, so much to read in Shirley Hughes' books." *Children's Books of the Year*

0-7445-3652-9	*Bouncing*
0-7445-3654-5	*Chatting*
0-7445-3653-7	*Giving*
0-7445-3655-3	*Hiding*

£4.50 each

OUT AND ABOUT

Eighteen richly-illustrated poems portray the weather and activities associated with the various seasons.

"Hughes at her best. Simple, evocative rhymes conjure up images that then explode in the magnificent richness of her paintings." *The Guardian*

0-7445-1422-3   £4.99

TALES FROM TROTTER STREET

"Shirley Hughes is one of the all-time greats and her new series accurately describes the life of contemporary city kids." *Susan Hill, Today*

0-7445-2012-6	*Wheels* £4.99
0-7445-2032-0	*Angel Mae* £4.99
0-7445-2357-5	*The Snow Lady* £4.99
0-7445-2033-9	*The Big Concrete Lorry* £4.99